MIGHTY ROBOT

VS. THE MUTANT MOSQUITOES FROM MERCURY

STORY BY
DAV PILKEY

ART BY
DAN SANTAT

SCHOLASTIC INC.

FOR A.J., KATIE, JOSH, BECKY, AND ADAM BUTLER
– D.P.

FOR JODI
– D.S.

Text copyright © 2000, 2014 by Dav Pilkey
www.pilkey.com

Illustrations copyright © 2014 by Dan Santat
www.dantat.com

For information regarding permission, write to Scholastic Inc., Attention: Permissions Department, 557 Broadway, New York, NY 10012.

Library of Congress Cataloging-in-Publication Data

Pilkey, Dav, 1966 – author.
Ricky Ricotta's mighty robot vs. the mutant mosquitoes from Mercury /
story by Dav Pilkey ; art by Dan Santat. — Revised edition.
pages cm
Summary: A mouse named Ricky Ricotta and his giant flying robot attempt to save the world from an invasion of massive mutant mosquitoes from Mercury.
1. Ricotta, Ricky (Fictitious character) — Juvenile fiction. 2. Mice — Juvenile fiction. 3. Robots — Juvenile fiction. 4. Heroes — Juvenile fiction. 5. Mosquitoes — Juvenile fiction. 6. Mercury (Planet) — Juvenile fiction. [1. Mice — Fiction. 2. Robots — Fiction. 3. Heroes — Fiction. 4. Humorous stories.] I. Santat, Dan, illustrator. II. Pilkey, Dav, 1966 – Ricky Ricotta's giant robot vs. the mutant mosquitoes from Mercury. III. Title. IV. Title: Ricky Ricotta's mighty robot versus the mutant mosquitoes from Mercury.
PZ7.P63123Rs 2014   813.54 — dc23   2014003618

ISBN 978-0-545-63010-8

12 11 10 9 8 7 6 5 4 3 2   19 20 21 22 23/0

Printed in China   62

Revised edition
First printing, May 2014

Book design by Phil Falco

CHAPTERS

CHAPTER ONE
RICKY AND HIS ROBOT

There once was a mouse named Ricky Ricotta who lived in Squeakyville with his mother and father.

Ricky Ricotta might have been
the smallest mouse around . . .

. . . but he had the BIGGEST
best friend in town.

CHAPTER TWO
SCHOOL DAYS

Ricky and his Mighty Robot
liked to go to school together.

Sometimes when Ricky was running late, his Robot would fly him straight to the front door.

After school, the Mighty Robot liked to help Ricky with his homework. The Robot's computer brain could solve complex math problems . . .

. . . his finger had a built-in pencil
sharpener . . .

. . . and he could even remove his telescopic eyeball, which made studying the planets much easier.

"Wow," said Ricky. "I can see all the way to Mercury! That's cool!"

CHAPTER THREE
MR. MOSQUITO HATES MERCURY!

Mercury was the smallest planet in the solar system, and it was the closest planet to the sun. But it certainly was not *cool*!

Just ask Mr. Mosquito.
He lived on Mercury, and he
HATED everything about it!

He hated the long, *long*, HOT days. Each day on Mercury, the temperature rose to more than eight hundred degrees!

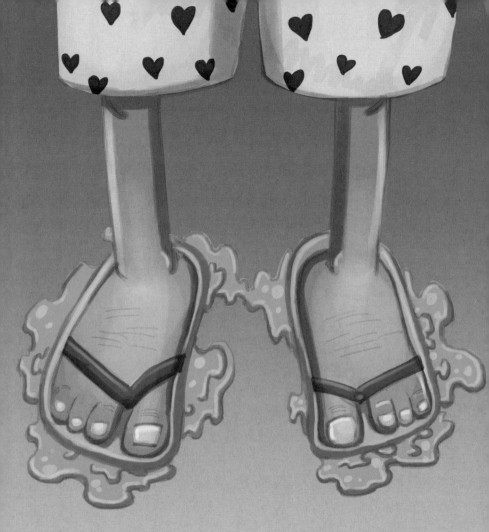

Mr. Mosquito couldn't even walk down the street because his flip-flops always melted on the sidewalk.

Mr. Mosquito hated Mercury's long, *long*, COLD nights, too. Each night on Mercury, the temperature dropped to almost three hundred degrees below zero!

Mr. Mosquito couldn't even brush his teeth because his toothpaste was always frozen solid!

"I've g-g-got to g-g-get away f-f-from th-th-this awful p-p-planet," said Mr. Mosquito, shivering in the cold. So Mr. Mosquito looked at his view screen and saw the planet Earth.

He saw mice playing happily on cool autumn days.

He saw them sleeping soundly on warm summer nights.

"Earth is the planet for me!" said Mr. Mosquito. "Soon it will be mine!"

CHAPTER FOUR
MR. MOSQUITO MAKES HIS MOVE

Mr. Mosquito went into his secret laboratory and clipped his filthy fingernails.

He put the clippings into a giant machine and zapped them with a powerful ray.

Then Mr. Mosquito's fingernails
grew and grew and grew . . .

. . . into massive Mutant Mosquitoes!
Mr. Mosquito climbed aboard his
spaceship and called to his troops.

"Mutant Mosquitoes," he cried,
"it is time to conquer Earth!
Follow me!"

And they did.

CHAPTER FIVE
THE MOSQUITOES ATTACK

When Mr. Mosquito got to Earth, he ordered his Mutant Mosquitoes to attack Squeakyville.

Ricky was in math class that afternoon. He looked out the window and saw the Mutant Mosquitoes.

"Uh-oh," said Ricky. "It looks like Squeakyville needs our help!"

Ricky raised his hand.

"May I be excused?" Ricky asked his teacher. "My Robot and I have to save the Earth."

"Not until you've finished your math test," said Ricky's teacher.

Ricky had three problems left. "What is two times three?" he asked himself aloud.

Ricky's Robot was waiting outside. He wanted to help. So he dashed to the teachers' parking lot and brought back some cars.

Ricky's Robot put three cars
into one pile, and he put three
cars into another pile.

Ricky looked at the piles of cars.
"*Two* piles of *three* cars," said
Ricky. "Two times three equals *six!*"

Ricky looked at his next question.
"What is *six* minus *five*?" he asked.
Ricky's Robot knew just what to do.

He threw five of the cars back
into the parking lot.

"I get it," said Ricky. "Six minus
five equals *one*!"

Ricky's last question was the hardest of all. "What is *one* divided by *two*?" he asked.

The Robot used his mighty karate chop to divide one car in two.

"That was easy," said Ricky. "One divided by two equals *one-half*!"

Ricky handed in his test. Then he climbed out the window.

"Let's go, Mighty Robot," said Ricky. "We've got to save the Earth."

"M-M-M-My *car!*" cried Ricky's teacher.

CHAPTER SIX
THE HEROES ARRIVE

Ricky and his Mighty Robot ran downtown to face the Mutant Mosquitoes.

The Mosquitoes attacked
Ricky's Robot.

"Hey," said Ricky. "Four against
one is not fair!"

Then Ricky had an idea. "Come with me, Robot," said Ricky.

The Mighty Robot was busy fighting, so he could not follow Ricky. But his arm could stretch very far!

Ricky and his Robot's arm stretched all the way to the Bugs Away bug-spray factory. Ricky told the Robot's arm to grab one of the huge bug-spray storage tanks.

BUGS AWAY

Then they headed back to the battle.

CHAPTER SEVEN
A BUGGY BATTLE

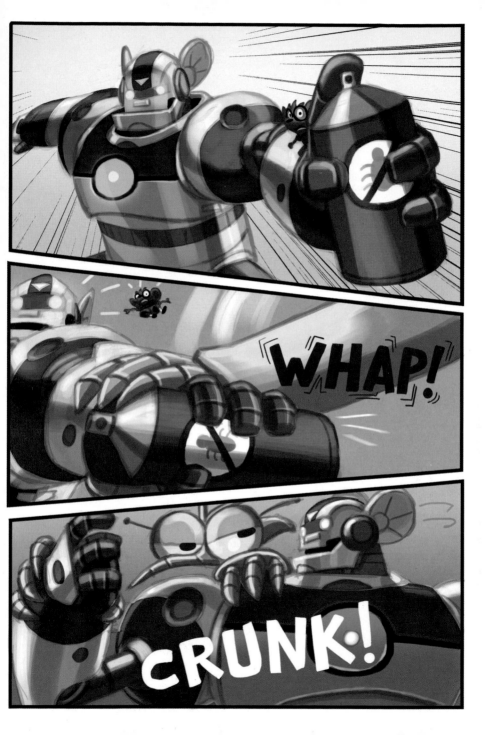

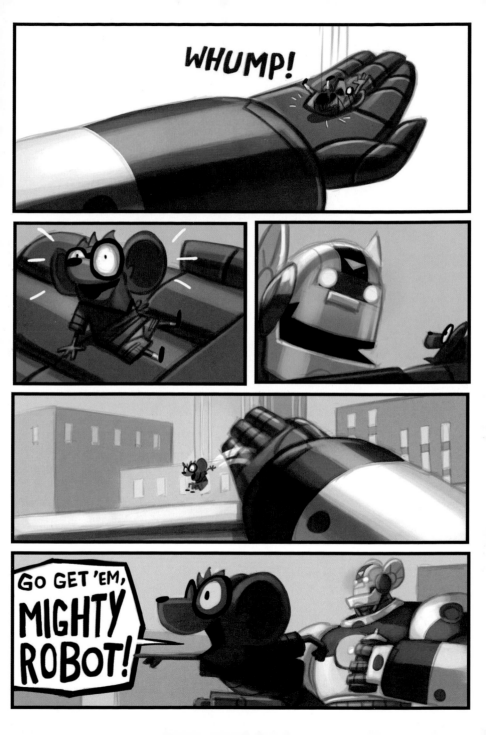

The Robot shook the tank of bug spray.

The Robot sprayed the Mosquitoes.

Then he broke up the buggy battle
with a big blast from his bionic boot!

CHAPTER EIGHT
MR. MOSQUITO'S REVENGE

The Mutant Mosquitoes had been
defeated. Ricky's Mighty Robot
chased them into space.

The Mosquitoes flew back
to Mercury and never bothered
anybody again.

Mr. Mosquito was very angry.
He grabbed Ricky and took him
into his spaceship. "Help me, Robot!"
Ricky cried.

But it was too late. Mr. Mosquito
chained Ricky up. Then he went to his
control panel and pulled a secret lever.

Suddenly, his spaceship began
to change. It shifted . . .

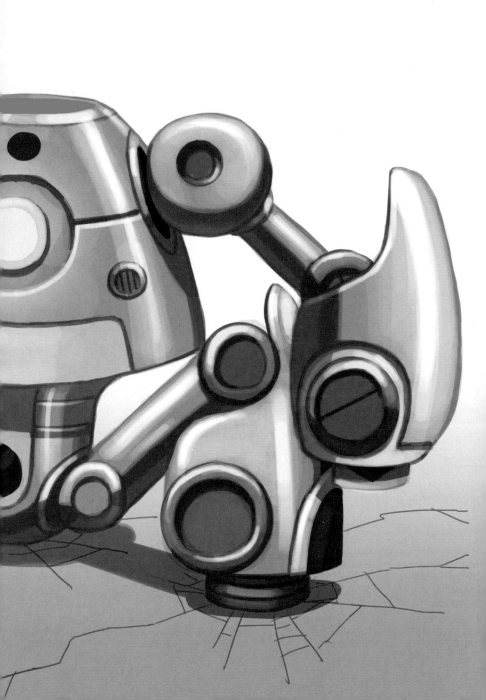

. . . and grew . . .

. . . and transformed into a giant
Mecha-Mosquito!

The Mecha-Mosquito attacked Ricky's
Mighty Robot. But Ricky's Robot would
not fight back.

He knew that Ricky was inside the Mecha-Mosquito, and he did not want his best friend to get hurt.

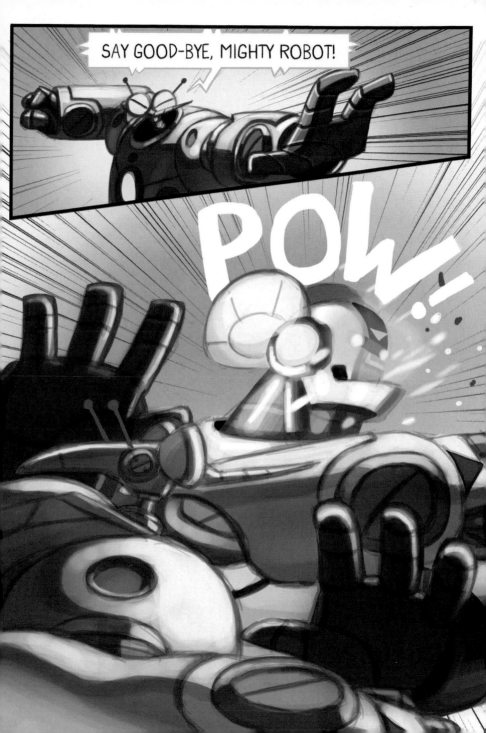

The Mecha-Mosquito pounded
Ricky's Robot.

What could Ricky do?

Ricky thought and thought. Then he had an idea.

"Mr. Mosquito," said Ricky, "I have to go to the bathroom."

"Not now," said Mr. Mosquito. "I am too busy beating up your Robot!"

"But it's an emergency," said Ricky.

"All right, all right," said Mr. Mosquito. He unlocked Ricky's chains and led him to the boys' room.

"Hurry up in there!" he yelled.

Inside the bathroom, Ricky opened a window and stuck his head outside.

"Pssssst!" Ricky whispered.

The Robot saw Ricky, and he held
out his giant hand.

Ricky jumped.

"I'm safe," said Ricky. "Now it will be a fair fight!"

CHAPTER NINE
RICKY'S ROBOT STRIKES BACK

Inside the Mecha-Mosquito, Mr. Mosquito was getting very angry. He knocked on the bathroom door. "Let's hurry up in there!" he yelled. "I haven't got all da—"

KER-POW!

Ricky's Robot punched the Mecha-Mosquito right in the face.

Mr. Mosquito leaped to his control panel and fought back hard. The final battle was about to begin.

CHAPTER TEN
THE FINAL BATTLE
(IN FLIP-O-RAMA™)

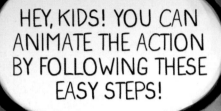

-RAMA
HERE'S HOW IT WORKS!

STEP 1
Place your *left* hand inside the dotted lines marked "LEFT HAND HERE." Hold the book open *flat*.

STEP 2
Grasp the *right-hand* page with your right thumb and index finger (inside the dotted lines marked "RIGHT THUMB HERE").

STEP 3
Now *quickly* flip the right-hand page back and forth until the picture appears to be *animated*.

(For extra fun, try adding your own sound-effects!)

FLIP-O-RAMA 1

(pages 97 and 99)

Remember, flip *only* page 97.
While you are flipping, be sure you
can see the picture on page 97
and the one on page 99.
If you flip quickly, the two
pictures will start to look like
<u>one</u> *animated* picture.

Don't forget to add
your own sound-effects!

LEFT HAND HERE

THE MECHA-MOSQUITO ATTACKED.

RIGHT
THUMB
HERE

RIGHT
INDEX
FINGER
HERE

THE MECHA-MOSQUITO
ATTACKED.

FLIP-O-RAMA 2

(pages 101 and 103)

Remember, flip *only* page 101.
While you are flipping, be sure you
can see the picture on page 101
and the one on page 103.
If you flip quickly, the two
pictures will start to look like
<u>one</u> *animated* picture.

Don't forget to add
your own sound-effects!

LEFT HAND HERE

RICKY'S ROBOT
FOUGHT BACK.

RIGHT
THUMB
HERE

RIGHT
INDEX
FINGER
HERE

102

**RICKY'S ROBOT
FOUGHT BACK.**

FLIP-O-RAMA 3

(pages 105 and 107)

Remember, flip only page 105.
While you are flipping, be sure you
can see the picture on page 105
and the one on page 107.
If you flip quickly, the two
pictures will start to look like
one animated picture.

Don't forget to add
your own sound-effects!

LEFT HAND HERE

THE MECHA-MOSQUITO
BATTLED HARD.

THE MECHA-MOSQUITO BATTLED HARD.

FLIP-O-RAMA 4

(pages 109 and 111)

Remember, flip *only* page 109.
While you are flipping, be sure you
can see the picture on page 109
and the one on page 111.
If you flip quickly, the two
pictures will start to look like
<u>one</u> *animated* picture.

Don't forget to add
your own sound-effects!

LEFT HAND HERE

RICKY'S ROBOT
BATTLED HARDER.

RIGHT
THUMB
HERE

RICKY'S ROBOT
BATTLED HARDER.

FLIP-O-RAMA 5

(pages 113 and 115)

Remember, flip *only* page 113.
While you are flipping, be sure you
can see the picture on page 113
and the one on page 115.
If you flip quickly, the two
pictures will start to look like
<u>one</u> *animated* picture.

Don't forget to add
your own sound-effects!

LEFT HAND HERE

RICKY'S ROBOT
SAVED THE DAY!

113

RICKY'S ROBOT
SAVED THE DAY!

CHAPTER ELEVEN
JUSTICE PREVAILS

The Mecha-Mosquito had been destroyed, and Ricky Ricotta's Mighty Robot was victorious.

Mr. Mosquito crawled out of his damaged ship and began to cry. "What a bad day I am having!" cried Mr. Mosquito.

"It's about to get worse," said Ricky.

Ricky's Mighty Robot picked up
Mr. Mosquito and dropped him into
the Squeakyville jail.

Then Ricky and his Mighty Robot
flew home for chocolate milk and
grilled cheese sandwiches.

"You boys have saved the world again," said Ricky's mother.

"Yes," said Ricky's father. "Thank you for sticking together and fighting for what was right!"

"No problem," said Ricky . . .

. . . "that's what friends are for."

RICKY RICOTTA
AND HIS MIGHTY ROBOT
ARE BEST BUDDIES – BUT WITH BIG FRIENDS COME BIG RESPONSIBILITIES. . . .

Find out what happens when Ricky's parents decide to teach the boys a lesson about being responsible in their next adventure, *Ricky Ricotta's Mighty Robot vs. the Voodoo Vultures from Venus!*

READY FOR

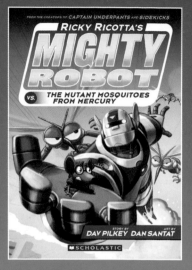

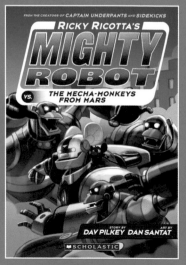

MORE RICKY?

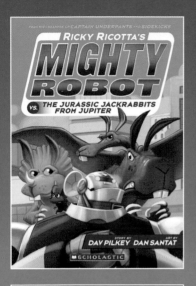

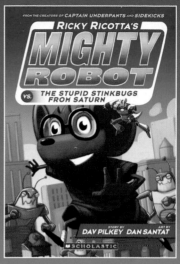

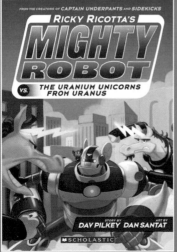

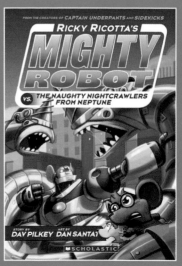

DAV PILKEY

has written and illustrated more than fifty books for children, including *The Paperboy*, a Caldecott Honor book; *Dog Breath: The Horrible Trouble with Hally Tosis*, winner of the California Young Reader Medal; and the IRA Children's Choice Dumb Bunnies series. He is also the creator of the *New York Times* bestselling Captain Underpants books. Dav lives in the Pacific Northwest with his wife. Find him online at www.pilkey.com.

DAN SANTAT

is the writer and illustrator of the picture book *The Adventures of Beekle: The Unimaginary Friend*. He is also the creator of the graphic novel *Sidekicks* and has illustrated many acclaimed picture books, including the *New York Times* bestseller *Because I'm Your Dad* by Ahmet Zappa and *Crankenstein* by Samantha Berger. Dan also created the Disney animated hit *The Replacements*. He lives in Southern California with his family. Find him online at www.dantat.com.